Fancy Aunt Jess

WRITTEN BY

AMY HEST

ILLUSTRATED BY

AMY SCHWARTZ

MORROW JUNIOR BOOKS/NEW YORK

For Aunt Gloria, who's a little bit fancy too
A.H.

For Anne
A.S.

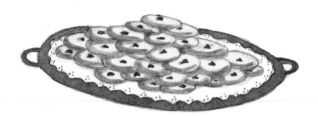

Text copyright © 1990 by Amy Hest

Illustrations copyright © 1990 by Amy Schwartz

Printed in Singapore at Tien Wah Press.

1 2 3 4 5 6 7 8 9 10

Library of Congress Cataloging-in-Publication Data
Hest, Amy.
Fancy Aunt Jess / Amy Hest : pictures by Amy Schwartz.
p.   cm.
Summary: A girl enjoys being with her unmarried Aunt Jess, who lives in Brooklyn.
ISBN 0-688-08096-0—ISBN 0-688-08097-9 (lib. bdg.)
[1. Aunts—Fiction.   2. Jews—United States—Fiction.   3. Brooklyn
(New York, N.Y.)—Fiction.]   I. Schwartz, Amy, ill.   II. Title.
PZ7.H4375Fan   1990
[E]—dc19   88-34370   CIP   AC

I have an aunt who is really my mother's cousin. This makes her my second cousin, I think. I call her Fancy Aunt Jess. Whenever she comes to our house, she takes the train. It is always late. We meet her at the station and I run along the platform waving at faces in windows until I see hers.

Now when Fancy Aunt Jess steps off a train, people take a look. And why not? She's the grandest lady around.

"Becky!" she calls, holding her hat against the wind. She always wears a hat with a wide brim and a wide grosgrain ribbon wrapped around the middle. It looks like a man's hat but Aunt Jess looks nothing like a man!

"New shoes? I like them," I say, inspecting those skinny high heels that click when she walks.

On the way home I sit squeezed between her and my mother. They talk and laugh, laugh and talk, and whisper things that sound like secrets. My mother never forgets to ask Aunt Jess about the men in her life.

The usual question is this: "How's the man in your life?"

And the usual answer is this: "Oh! He's a charmer, a very lovely fellow."

Then, from my mother: "So, will you marry this one?"

"Not on your life! Something is missing," explains Aunt Jess. "I can't say *what*, but something isn't there."

Later I stand around the kitchen watching them pour, and pour, from the porcelain coffeepot. The minute Aunt Jess slips out of her shoes, I slip into them, and I touch the warm fur that lines the sleeves of her coat.

But nothing is quite as grand as a sleepover in her city apartment. Aunt Jess meets me at Grand Central Terminal. The train from our house comes in on Track Number 12, and she is always waiting and waving at the top of the ramp.

"Can we ride the double-decker, *please*!" I beg.

Aunt Jess snaps up my plaid valise, leading me outside to the bright sunshine and to Fifth Avenue where the shiny yellow and green buses are lined up all in a row.

Afterward, we go underground to the dimly lit subway. We sit on yellow woven seats and take this train they call the Number 2 train all the way to Brooklyn.

Now when it comes to walking, Aunt Jess does it faster than anyone I know. It's hard to keep up as we scoot down busy Brooklyn streets, stopping in this shop, then that one, choosing things for dinner.

"Chicken legs! I saved these for you," says Mr. Levy, the butcher. He wears a white coat like a doctor's coat, and he whistles a funny tune when Aunt Jess sweeps across his sawdust floor.

"New coat?" asks Mrs. Levy, perched on a tall stool behind the chicken counter.

Aunt Jess spins around twice to the right. Then once again, left. "Do you like it, Mrs. Levy?"

The butcher's wife grunts. "You should wear it in good health," she says, "and you should find a husband."

"Someday maybe!" Aunt Jess laughs as she gathers up her packages.

Finally we turn onto her quiet block. Here the houses are set back from the street and the trees are tall like country trees, making high green arches overhead. Aunt Jess's apartment is on the top floor of Mrs. Mott's house. Number 1645.

We climb and climb the winding stairs.
"When *will* you get married?" I ask as we go.
"Don't know, Becky."
"Don't you ever fall in love?"
"Sometimes," she says, "but it only lasts awhile."

"Well, how does it *feel*?"

"Really fine," she says. "Like a birthday but better."

"Better than *that*?" I take a seat, right where I am on the top step.

"Better than *that*." Aunt Jess bunches up her pleated skirt. She sits, too, and stretches her legs down a few steps. "But the man I marry, he will be special."

"Special how?" I say.

"I don't quite know," she admits with a sigh. "But one thing is certain, he'll give me goose bumps, Becky."

"Is that all?"

Aunt Jess smiles. "Goose bumps are enough for me."

After dinner we carry cups of tea to the soft blue couch. Aunt Jess snips strings on the box that says Best Brooklyn Bakery, and she hands me a cookie that is really two cookies with raspberry jelly in the middle. Then we watch the night. The Brooklyn sky is black all right, but across the river city lights blink away, making jagged lines up and down the water. And every now and then we hear a gentle *put-put* of a barge or boat.

"When I grow up," I tell Aunt Jess, "I will have my own apartment, too. It's going to be just like yours with rows of books in shelves and wide windows so I can watch the boats at night."

"Maybe we'll be neighbors, Becky."

"What about that special man," I say, "the one who gives you goose bumps?"

"What about him?"

"Do you think he'll mind if we are neighbors?"

"*Him*? He won't mind. Not a bit." Aunt Jess smiles. "We three will take long bike rides on Sunday mornings and we'll picnic near the river. I'll bring cookies from our favorite bakery...."

"And you and I will tell secrets like crazy." I snuggle close to Aunt Jess. Her puffy quilt toasts our toes and sometimes I fall asleep. Just like that.

Friday night sleepovers are best. As the sun sinks down and down, Aunt Jess and I walk—slower this time—along quiet streets to the temple. She looks prettier than ever in her narrow blue dress and the long string of pearls and her red Friday night hat.

I love sitting beside her in the big old shul, watching her watch the rabbi. We always sit on the side near the colored-glass windows. The rabbi talks. He talks and talks but I don't mind. He reminds me of my grandfather, who had white hair like his and a kind voice, too. Sometimes the rabbi looks over at me and he smiles. Maybe I remind him of someone, too.

One Friday night I notice someone new, a girl with a
red-brown braid like mine. She's across the aisle and one seat
over, where I can watch every single thing she does. Mostly she is
squirming, and in her bright red sweater, she looks hotter even
than me. Beside her is a tall man with curly black hair and a silky
white shawl with fringe on the bottom. She looks nice, that girl,
and I think she knows I'm watching.

I nudge Aunt Jess. "There's a new girl," I whisper.

"Her braid reminds me of your braid, Becky."

"Do you think that's her father?" I ask.

"Don't know." Aunt Jess fidgets with her white cloth gloves.

They close at the wrist with tiny pearl buttons.

Next time I go to the shul, I look for the girl again. She isn't there and I am mad. But the *next* time she is! Squirming away in that hot red sweater.

"She's back!" I say, excited.

"Shhh."

"The tall man," I say, stretching my neck for a better look, "he's handsome."

"*Shhhhhh.*" Aunt Jess blushes. And not just a little blush, either. She rubs her arms, too, as if she were cold.

The rabbi makes a coughing noise that means Quiet Please, and people in the front rows twist around to frown at us. The girl twists, too, and the man-who-is-handsome. Now when *he* takes a look at Aunt Jess, he doesn't frown. Not one little bit!

"He likes you," I whisper.

Aunt Jess looks down at the book in her lap.

Afterward, ladies from the temple serve cookies and squares of cake and red wine in paper cups. I squeeze around a clump of grown-ups to get to the cookie table. My favorites are the ones with sprinkles. There are never enough.

"These ladies bring too much sponge cake." It's the girl with the red-brown braid! "Your mother is pretty," she says. "My name is Nicole."

"I am Becky and she isn't my mother. *That* is Aunt Jess. Fancy Aunt Jess."

I give a little wave to Aunt Jess across the room.

"And *that*," says Nicole, "is my Uncle Harry. He's special."

"Special how?" I say.

Nicole shrugs. "He just is."

I watch her Uncle Harry watching Aunt Jess. And I rub my arms, too, as if I were cold.

"He likes her," decides Nicole. "Maybe they'll get married."

"Married! *Her*?" I laugh. And I think about the goose bumps.

"Someday maybe."

And someday soon—they do.